MAURICE MINOR

D1329342

Story by
BARBARA HAYES

Illustrated by J.B. Long

OCTOPUS BOOKS

A RIDGMOUNT BOOK
First published 1986 by Octopus Books Ltd
59 Grosvenor Street, London W1

© 1986 Martspress Ltd
ISBN: 0 7064 2594 4

Produced by Mandarin Publishers Ltd
22a Westlands Road
Quarry Bay, Hong Kong

Printed in Hong Kong

M aurice Minor is a reliable little blue car who lived a quiet life in the countryside with elderly Mrs Conway. This is the story of how Maurice moved to town and began an exciting new life filled with adventures.

Maurice Minor, the little blue car, set out one lovely Spring morning with his owner, Mrs Conway. 'Shopping as usual, I suppose,' he thought.

They left their whitewashed cottage and drove between old stone walls towards the main road.

'Munch! Munch! Munch!' called Maurice to the sheep, grazing with their lambs in the field. 'Don't you get bored with eating grass all day?'

'No. BAAA!' replied the sheep. 'Don't you get bored with chugging round the same old roads?'

Maurice never did get bored with chugging round the roads of the Lake District, where he and Mrs Conway lived. However on that day, to his surprise, instead of driving to the shops, Mrs Conway went on a long trip to visit her son and grandchildren.

'How pretty the flowering cherry trees are at this time of the year,' thought Maurice, as they drew up outside the house where the younger Conways lived.

'Hallo, Grandma. Hallo, Maurice,' called Harry, running out to meet them.

Mrs Conway's visit lasted several days. Then, to Maurice's amazement, she said to him: 'Maurice, I have decided to give you to Harry. I am sure it is a surprise and you must not be upset. Harry has just passed his driving test and needs a well-balanced little car to help him gain more experience. A big powerful car could be dangerous for him. You will be able to help him a great deal.'

Harry was just as surprised, and thrilled too. 'Oh thank you, Grandma. My very own car!' he beamed.

Maurice was not sure whether to be pleased or upset. He liked Harry, but would he like his new home?

Harry and Maurice drove Mrs Conway to the railway station and put her on a train back to the Lake District.

'Goodbye, Grandma and thanks again for Maurice,' shouted Harry to Mrs Conway, who waved from her carriage.

Maurice stood neatly between the white lines in the station car park. He felt quite excited.

'I did like living away in the quiet countryside,' thought Maurice, 'but I suppose it was rather dull. Down here in this big town, things should be much more exciting and lively.'

Harry reversed Maurice, then drove carefully towards the car park exit where two of his friends saw him. 'Harry!' they shouted, hammering on Maurice's roof. 'What are you doing in that car?'

'It's mine!' Harry boasted very proudly, stopping and getting out. 'Isn't it great!'

'Oh, NO!' groaned Maurice. He knew that Harry should not have stopped in the exit from the busy station car park, but no matter how much he revved and coughed, the boys took no notice.

'How marvellous! You *are* lucky! Will you take us for a ride?' burbled the friends.

'TOOT! TOOT! Out of the way please!' hooted an angry red car, pressing up behind them.

'You don't *own* the car park, you know," screeched an impatient saloon behind that, hooting noisily.

Harry hastened out of the station car park and drove Maurice carefully home. 'I can drive,' he said, 'but I still have a lot to learn. You will have to be patient with me, Maurice.'

'Very well,' chugged Maurice, in agreement.

There was no room for Maurice in the family garage and he spent a lot of time standing in the driveway. He became friendly with the big, brown dog, Saxon, who lived next door.

'Good morning,' Saxon would bark over the fence.

One day Maurice overheard Harry chatting to Saxon and George Carter, who lived next door with his father.

'I am not going to live here any more,' George was saying. 'I hate town life and have bought a little farm in the country. I am going to move there and take Saxon with me. He is too big for Dad to manage on his own. The country will be just the place for him.'

Maurice felt very doubtful. He knew how much Saxon loved old Mr Carter, George's father.

Needless to say, George did not ask Maurice's opinion about the move, and a few days later he put Saxon into the back of his car and drove off to his farm in the country.

Old Mr Carter waved goodbye from in front of his house, while Saxon stared forlornly from the rear window of George's red car.

'No good will come of this,' thought Maurice, 'no matter how nice that farm is, nor how kind young George tries to be.'

The days went by. Maurice led a very happy life with Harry, but he heard that Saxon could not settle in the country and was moping. Finally, George sent word that Saxon had disappeared altogether. No one could find him.

Then, one morning at dawn, Maurice opened sleepy eyes to see a thin, scruffy, exhausted dog limping past the front gate. It was Saxon!

As Maurice watched, the bedraggled dog fell to the ground, too hungry and thirsty to go a step further!

'Poor Saxon has found his way home,' thought Maurice. Then he began to feel anxious. Saxon lay on the cold, hard pavement without moving.

Taking a deep breath, Maurice forced a TOOT TOOT from his horn.

Lights went on in the houses, then Harry came running out to see what was wrong. Old Mr Carter looked from his window.

'It's Saxon!' Harry called out. 'He's in a terrible state. You had better come down, Mr Carter.'

Somehow, brave Saxon had found his way for miles and miles to reach his former home and master.

Old Mr Carter nursed the faithful dog back to health and promised that he would never be sent away again. Maurice felt very pleased.

However, Mr Carter was not as young as he used to be and on the days when he did not feel like walking, Harry and Maurice took Saxon for long romps on the hills.

'You're a real friend, Maurice,' woofed Saxon.

Spring gave way to Summer, and Maurice became quite a busy little town car. He loved the excitement of running round with Harry and his young friends.

Then a very important day arrived. It was Harry's first day at work. His father bought him a proper suit. His mother gave him a white office shirt and a new tie. Mrs Conway sent a smart briefcase. Maurice waited outside, polished and spotless.

'Looking smart for business is very important,' said Harry's parents, as they saw him off.

It was Maurice's job to drive Harry to and from work every day. On that first morning, they arrived early to make a good impression. They went into the car park behind the office block where Harry was to work.

'I wonder if this is right?' thought Maurice. 'All these parking slots are numbered, and I don't know which number is for me.'

Then they noticed the gatekeeper running out of his hut, calling to them. 'Come back!' he shouted.

Harry parked Maurice neatly and got out, watched by the other cars. 'I know this is a private car park for people who work in the offices,' he said politely to the gatekeeper, 'but don't worry. I have just started to work here. This is my first day.'

'That may be,' replied the gatekeeper, 'but you still cannot park here. These parking slots are for *important* members of the staff, not newcomers like you. You must park your car out in the street, until you have worked your way up in the company.'

Feeling very small, Harry and Maurice slunk out of the car park and found a place at the side of the road. At lunch time Harry went to see if Maurice was well.

'Sorry, old chap,' he said, patting the car. 'I know it's noisy and dirty here, but what can I do?'

Maurice smiled bravely although his head ached.

At that moment, an elderly gentleman stopped to admire Maurice. 'Fine little car!' he said, 'but you shouldn't leave it parked in this busy road all day. It might get knocked by a passing lorry.'

'Oh, I know,' agreed Harry. 'I hate leaving him here, but I have just started work in those offices and there is no room for Maurice in the car park.'

'Nonsense!' said the elderly gentleman. 'Of course there is room for a well-kept little thoroughbred like this. I once had one like him myself. Come with me, I own all this property.'

So saying he strode off to find the gatekeeper. In no time at all a space was cleared.

'What a stroke of luck!' thought Harry.

So, the first day at work was a big success. Maurice had a snug parking spot and Harry managed to please his employers with his work.

But the very next morning – oh dear! The postman brought a letter saying that Maurice needed a new tax disc. Maurice had to pass his Ministry of Transport test!

'Maurice!' gasped Harry. 'I forgot that you were old and needed testing! What a nuisance! You must go for a test immediately, or I cannot drive you any more.'

Poor Harry had to miss his breakfast and rush off to the office by bus. He did not want to be late on his second day at work.

His mother had to abandon all the jobs she wanted to do and drive Maurice to the garage to be tested. She handed the car keys to a mechanic.

'He is a sound little car,' she said. 'I am sure there is nothing wrong.'

'That's what they all say,' sighed the mechanic, as he took Maurice into the testing shed.

Of course, Maurice had been for tests before, but that had been with his old friend, Mr Handyspanner at the local 'Keep 'em Rolling' garage in the Lake District. This big town garage seemed rather tough and heartless.

Maurice gritted his teeth. 'I *will* pass, for Harry's sake,' he thought.

He stopped and started his engine, and shone his headlamps and flicked his indicator light exactly when asked. In no time at all Maurice passed his test.

So, Maurice got his new tax disc and soon it was time for the summer holidays. Harry decided to go away with his friend from the office, Bobby.

'Let's go camping for a few days,' suggested Harry, 'and then on to stay with my grandma.'

Maurice was very pleased. 'It will be lovely to see my old owner, Mrs Conway, again,' he thought.

They set off towards the Lake District, past the familiar green fields surrounded by low stone walls.

'Just like old times,' chugged Maurice Minor.

Neither Harry nor his friend, Bobby, knew very much about camping. They left it till almost nightfall before they tried to find a place to pitch their tent.

Luckily, as the shadows were lengthening, they came to a farm. Harry pulled up in the farmyard and went to speak to the farmer. 'You may camp in the second meadow on the right, down the lane,' he said, 'and be careful to close the gate behind you.'

Bobby yawned sleepily. Maurice felt tired too, he had driven a long way that day.

Harry climbed back into the driving seat and nosed Maurice down the lane. 'Second meadow on the left,' he sighed. 'What a kind farmer! I'm too tired to drive another inch.'

'On the left. On the left?' queried Maurice to himself. 'I could have sworn the farmer said "on the right". Oh well, I must have been mistaken, I suppose.' But Maurice had not been mistaken.

On they went down the lane, for quite a long way till they found the gate into the second meadow.

By the time Harry and Bobby had unpacked their new red tent, the daylight was completely gone. Luckily a full moon was shining brightly, and they could just see enough to put up the tent. Then, exhausted, they clambered into their sleeping bags and fell asleep. Maurice closed his eyes, thankful that the long day and the long journey were all past.

Suddenly SCREECH! WHOOSH! An express train thundered by. Nothing could sleep through all that noise! The trains roared past all night long.

Poor Maurice hardly slept a wink and neither did the boys. As the sun rose, they were glad to get up. A brown and white cow came to look at them.

'MOOOO!' she said over the wall. 'You are camping in the wrong field. That field is far too noisy.'

'A pity you could not have told us that last night,' groaned Maurice. 'And now would you mind not mooing quite so loudly. I have rather a bad headache.'

Harry and Bobby managed to cook a nice breakfast, then, after thanking the farmer, they went on their way.

The sun was shining and Maurice tried to roll merrily along the road, but he was too sleepy to do his best. The boys were tired too.

'I think we had better call today a rest day after that bad night,' said Harry. He drove down to a sandy beach and left Maurice safely parked while he and Bobby went to doze near the sea.

'This is a *real* holiday,' smiled Maurice, as the seagulls circled overhead, families played in the sun, and yachts and a big ship sailed by.

Maurice and Bobby and Harry all fell into a deep sleep. SCREEEECH! Hours later the calling of a seagull woke Maurice with a start. He looked towards the beach and gasped with alarm.

The families had all gone. Only Harry and Bobby were still lying on the sand. The tide was coming in fast and the waves of cold water were about to wash over the boys and their belongings.

'TOOOOT! TOOOOT! *TOOOOOOT*!' shrieked Maurice. Just in time the boys woke up.

What a narrow escape! Harry and Bobby were glad to scramble back into Maurice and scuttle on their way. That night they went to a proper camping site, before heading off to visit Harry's grandma.

'Here is Mrs Conway's lane,' revved Maurice, as they reached the turning he had driven up so often with Harry's grandma. He looked fondly at the sheep, the cow and her calf, the girls on horseback, the hikers, the load of yellow hay. It was lovely to be back!

But Harry drove on without stopping!

'Why aren't we visiting Mrs Conway?' gasped Maurice, stalling and trying to turn back.

'I don't know what's come over Maurice,' said Harry. 'He doesn't usually play up like this.'

On they drove to the next town, where Harry pulled up outside a pretty little house. What a surprise! There was Mrs Conway, waving at them. And there was the old cat, Mouser, too.

'How do you like my new home, Maurice?' she called. So that was it! Mrs Conway had moved!

The boys unloaded and went inside. Mrs Conway stayed to show Maurice a present she had bought.

'I hadn't the heart to choose another car after I gave you to Harry,' smiled Mrs Conway. 'So I came to live here in the middle of town, where I didn't need to drive. But I often think about you and I have bought you these nice new seat covers, as a present.'

Maurice was so pleased. He loved his exciting new life with Harry, but it was nice to think Mrs Conway still remembered him. *He* would never forget *her*!

Other books in the series:

MICKY THE MG
Cheeky Micky the MG is bought by a collector of classic cars. Join him in his scrapes with Richard the Rolls and the short-tempered Sir 'Smart' Alec Smoothdeal.

BERTIE THE BENTLEY
Join Bertie the Bentley as he escapes the clutches of Mr Oilygrin the malicious mechanic and bravely saves a man's life by driving through perilous snowdrifts.

FREDDY THE FORD
Fortunate Freddy the Ford is rescued from a hire car's life of drudgery by a rich adventurer. Join them on their exciting escapades in exotic locations around the world.